Dear Parent:

Congratulations! Your child is taking the first steps on an exciting journey. The destination? Independent reading!

STEP INTO READING® will help your child get there. The program offers five steps to reading success. Each step includes fun stories and colorful art. There are also Step into Reading Sticker Books, Step into Reading Math Readers, Step into Reading Write-In Readers, Step into Reading Phonics Readers, and Step into Reading Phonics First Steps! Boxed Sets—a complete literacy program with something for every child.

Learning to Read, Step by Step!

Ready to Read   Preschool–Kindergarten
• big type and easy words • rhyme and rhythm • picture clues
For children who know the alphabet and are eager to begin reading.

Reading with Help   Preschool–Grade 1
• basic vocabulary • short sentences • simple stories
For children who recognize familiar words and sound out new words with help.

Reading on Your Own   Grades 1–3
• engaging characters • easy-to-follow plots • popular topics
For children who are ready to read on their own.

Reading Paragraphs   Grades 2–3
• challenging vocabulary • short paragraphs • exciting stories
For newly independent readers who read simple sentences with confidence.

Ready for Chapters   Grades 2–4
• chapters • longer paragraphs • full-color art
For children who want to take the plunge into chapter books but still like colorful pictures.

STEP INTO READING® is designed to give every child a successful reading experience. The grade levels are only guides. Children can progress through the steps at their own speed, developing confidence in their reading, no matter what their grade.

Remember, a lifetime love of reading starts with a single step!

For Smarty Anna, with love
—A.J.H.

To Sophia, who writes so well
—S.W.

Text copyright © 2008 by Anna Jane Hays
Illustrations copyright © 2008 by Sylvie Wickstrom

Published in the United States by Random House Children's Books, a division of Random House, Inc., New York.

Step into Reading, Random House, and the Random House colophon are registered trademarks of Random House, Inc.

www.stepintoreading.com

Educators and librarians, for a variety of teaching tools, visit us at
www.randomhouse.com/teachers

Library of Congress Cataloging-in-Publication Data
Hays, Anna Jane.
Smarty Sara / by Anna Jane Hays ; illustrated by Sylvie Wickstrom. — 1st ed.
    p.   cm. — (Step into reading. Step 2)
Summary: Everywhere Sara goes she brings along her journal where she jots notes, makes lists, draws pictures and maps, writes poems, and plans a big surprise for her friends.
ISBN 978-0-375-83512-4 (trade pbk.) — ISBN 978-0-375-95054-4 (lib. bdg.)
[1. Diaries—Fiction.] I. Kantorovitz, Sylvie, ill. II. Title.
PZ7.H314917Sm 2008 [E]—dc22 2007011068

Printed in the United States of America   10 9 8 7 6 5 4 3 2 1

First Edition

Smarty Sara

by Anna Jane Hays
illustrated by Sylvie Wickstrom

Random House 🏠 New York

Sara is so smart.

She keeps a book

for her writing.

She keeps it

for her art.

She writes her name
at the start.
Smarty Sara!

Sara finds a key
from her friend
next door.
She knows
what it is for!

Sara wants to show it.
Sara wants to share it.

She makes a plan.

She makes a list.

She jams everything
into her fat backpack.

Then it is time to scram.

It is time

to go meet Sam!

Sara takes her book
everywhere she goes.

She writes about
the things she knows.

MY DOG SANDY
I teach my dog to sit
and stand.
It tickles when
he licks my hand!
We live in SANDY LAND.

Sara draws in her book.

She draws what she sees.

Look!

Balloon trees!

Here comes Sam!

He wears a frown.

Sam asks,

"What is that key?"

Sara says,

"Wait and see!"

Now Sam's frown
turns upside down.

Sara and Sam
write a note.
They write the facts.
They invite Max.

Dear Max,
We have a surprise!
Read the CLUES.
Come to the gate.
Meet us at noon.
Do not be late!
Sara Sam

17

They take the note
to Max's door.
They knock and knock
and knock some more.

Max's sister Kate asks,

"What is that key?"

Sara says,

"Wait and see!"

Sara and Sam

make a map.

PARK

STORE

STOP

THE END

Sam writes clues
with yellow chalk.
He writes the clues
on the sidewalk.

Sam and Sara wait
and wait.
They play tic-tac-toe
by the gate.
It is noon!
Will Max come soon?

Where is Max?

"HERE I AM!"

"Yay!" shouts Sam.

Max asks Sara,

"What is that key?"

Sara says,

"You will see.

It is the

SECRET GARDEN key!"

"We can come in now!"

"Wow!"

"Bow-wow!"

Then Sara spreads out
her surprise.
A garden picnic
is the prize!

Sara smiles.
She takes a look
and writes about it
in her book.

Smarty Sara!